Photoset in 18/26pt Bembo by Goodfellow & Egan Ltd, Cambridge
Printed in Belgium by Proost International Book Production

British Library Cataloguing in Publication Data available

ISBN 0 7500 1498 9

Dick King-Smith

The Excitement of Being Ernest

Illustrated by Nigel McMullen

MACDONALD YOUNG BOOKS

Chapter One

The first thing that struck you about Ernest was his colour. If you had to put a name to it, you would say "honey" – not that pale wax honey that needs a knife to get it out of a jar, but the darker, richer, runny stuff that drips all over the tablecloth if you don't wind the spoon round it properly.

That was the colour of Ernest's coat, and the second thing about him that was remarkable was the amount of coat he carried. He was very hairy. Body, legs, tail, all had their fair share of that runny-honey-coloured hair. But it was Ernest's facé that was his fortune, with its fine beard and moustaches framed by shortish droopy ears.

From under bushy
eyebrows Ernest looked
out upon the world and
found it good.

Only one thing
bothered him. He did
not know what kind
of dog he was.

Chapter Two

It should have been simple, of course, to find out. There were a number of other dogs living in the village who could presumably have told him, but somehow Ernest had never plucked up the courage to ask.

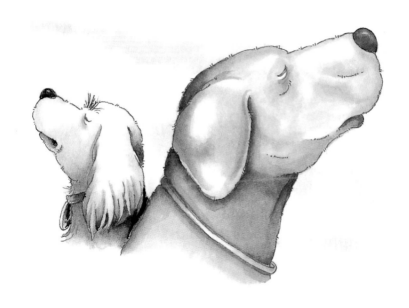

To begin with, the other dogs all looked so posh. They were all of different breeds, but each one appeared so obviously well-bred, so self-assured, so upper-class, that Ernest had always hesitated to approach them, least of all with a daft question like, "Excuse me. I wonder if you could tell me what sort of dog I am?"

For that matter, he thought to himself one day, I don't even know what sort of dogs they are, and then it occurred to him that that would be a much more sensible question to ask and could lead perhaps to the kind of conversation about breeds in general where one of them might say "I'm a Thingummytite, and you, I see, are a Wotchermecallum."

So after he had helped to get the cows
in for morning milking on the farm
where he lived, Ernest trotted up to the
village to the gateway of the Manor
House – an imposing entrance flanked
by fine pillars – and peered in through
his bushy eyebrows.

Standing in the drive was the Manor House dog.

Ernest lifted his leg politely on one of the fine stone pillars, and called out, "Excuse me! I wonder if you could tell me what sort of dog you are?"

"Ich bin ein German Short-haired Pointer," said the Manor House dog, "if dot is any business of yours."

"Oh," said Ernest. "I'm not one of those."

He waited expectantly to be told what he was.

"Dot," said the German Short-haired Pointer pointedly, "is as plain as der nose on your face," and he turned his back and walked away.

Ernest went on to the Vicarage, and saw, through the wicketgate, the Vicar's dog lying on the lawn.

"Excuse me," said Ernest, lifting his leg politely on the wicketgate. "I wonder if you could tell me what sort of dog you are?"

"Nom d'un chien!" said the Vicar's dog. "Je suis un French Bulldog."

"Oh," said Ernest. "I'm not one of those."

The French Bulldog snorted, and though Ernest waited hopefully for a while it said nothing more, so he walked down the road till he came to the pub.

The publican's dog was very large indeed, and Ernest thought it best to keep some distance away. He lifted his leg discreetly on an empty beer-barrel and shouted across the pub car-park, "Excuse me! I wonder if you could tell me what sort of dog you are?"

"Oi'm an Irish Wolfhound," said the publican's dog in a deep rumbly voice.

"Oh," said Ernest. "I'm not one of those."

"Bedad you're not," said the Irish Wolfhound. "Shall Oi be after tellin yez what sort of a dog ye are?"

"Oh, yes please," said Ernest eagerly.

"Sur ye're a misbegotton hairy mess," said the Irish Wolfhound, "and it's stinking of cow-muck ye are. Now bate it, if ye know what's good for you."

Ernest beat it. But he wasn't beaten.

He paid a call on a number of houses in the village street, repeating his polite enquiry and receiving answers of varying degrees of rudeness from a Tibetan Terrier, an American Cocker Spaniel, a Finnish Spitz, and a Chinese Crested Dog.

But none of them volunteered any information as to what kind of animal he himself was.

Chapter Three

There was one house left, by the
junction of the road with the lane that
led back to the farm, and standing
outside it was a dog that Ernest had
never seen before in the neighbourhood.

It looked friendly and wagged its long
plumy tail as Ernest left his customary
calling card on the gate.

"Hullo," he said. "I haven't seen you before."

"We've only just moved in," said the friendly stranger. "You're the first dog I've met here, actually. Are there a lot in the village?"

"Yes."

"Decent bunch?"

Ernest considered how best to answer this.

"They're all very well-bred," he said. "I imagine they've got pedigrees as long as your tail," he added, "like you have, I suppose?"

"You could say that," replied the other. "For what it's worth."

Ernest sighed. I'll give it one more go, he thought.

"Straight question," he said. "What sort of dog are you?"

"Straight answer. English Setter."

"English?" said Ernest delightedly.
"Well, that makes a change."

"How do you mean?"

"Why the rest of them are a pack of
foreigners. Chinese, German, Tibetan,
Irish, American, Finnish – there's no end
to the list."

"Really? No, no, I'm as English as
you are."

"Ah," said Ernest carefully. "Then you know what sort of dog I am?"

"Of course," said the English Setter. "You're a Gloucestershire Cow-dog."

The hair over Ernest's face prevented the Setter from seeing the changing expression that flitted across it, first of astonishment, then of excitement, and finally a studied look of smug satisfaction.

"Ah," said Ernest. "You knew. Not many do."

"My dear chap," said the Setter. "You amaze me. I should have thought any dog would have recognized a Gloucestershire Cow-dog immediately."

"Really?" said Ernest. "Well, I suppose any English dog would."

"Yes, that must be it. Anyway you'll be able to show all these foreign chaps, next week."

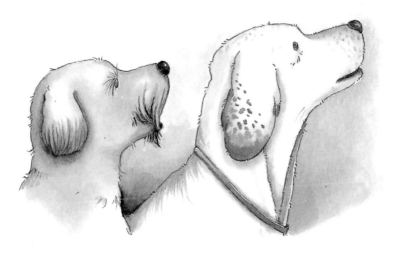

"Why, what's happening next week?"

"It's the Village Fete."

"Oh, I don't go to that sort of thing," said Ernest. "I've got too much work to do with the cows."

"Quite. But this year there's a new attraction, apparently. They've just put the posters up, haven't you seen?"

"Didn't notice," said Ernest.

"Well, there's one stuck on our wall. Come and have a look."

And this is what they saw.

VILLAGE FETE

Saturday June 15th

By kind permission, in the grounds
of the Manor House

★★★★★

Skittle Alley

Coconut Shy

Cake Stall

Jam and Preserve Stall

Hoopla

Wellie-throwing Competition

Guess the Weight of the Pig

Grand Dog Show

★★★★★

"But that's no good," said Ernest.
"With all the pedigree dogs in the
village, the judge will never look twice
at me."

26

Chapter Four

"But that's no good," said Sally. "With all the pedigree dogs in the village, the judge will never look twice at Ernest." Sally was the farmer's daughter, and she too was looking at another of the notices, tacked on the farm gate.

"Oh, I don't know," said her father. "You might be surprised. Have a go. It's only a bit of fun. You'll have to clean him up a bit, mind."

So when the great day dawned, Ernest ran to Sally's whistle after morning milking and found himself, to his surprise and disgust, required to stand in an old tin bath and be soaked and lathered and scrubbed and hosed, and then blow-dried with Sally's mother's electric drier plugged in to a power point in the dairy.

"He looks a treat," said the farmer and his wife when Sally had finished combing out that long honey-coloured coat. And he did.

Indeed when they all arrived at the Fete, a number of people had difficulty in recognizing Ernest without his usual covering of cow-muck.

But the dogs weren't fooled. Ernest heard them talking among themselves as the competitors began to gather for the Dog Show, and their comments made his head drop and his tail droop.

"Well I'll be goshdarned!" said the American Cocker Spaniel to the Tibetan Terrier. "Will ye look at that mutt! Kinda tough to have to share a show-ring with no-account trash like that?"

And, turning to the Finnish Spitz,
"Velly distlessing," said the Chinese
Crested Dog. "No pediglee."

"Ma foi!" said the French Bulldog to
the Irish Wolfhound.

"Regardez zis 'airy creature! 'E is, 'ow you say, mongrel?"

"Begorrah, it's the truth ye're spakin," said the Irish Wolfhound in his deep rumbly voice, "and it's stinking of soap powder he is."

As for the German Short-haired Pointer, he made sure, seeing that he was host for the day, that his comment on Ernest's arrival on the croquet-lawn (which was the show-ring) was heard by all.

"Velcome to der Manor, ladies and gentlemen," he said to the other dogs. "May der best-bred dog win," and he turned his back on Ernest in a very pointed way.

"Don't let them get you down, old chap," said a voice in Ernest's ear, and there, standing next to him, was the friendly English Setter, long plumy tail wagging.

"Oh, hullo," said Ernest in a doleful voice. "Nice to see you. I hope you win, anyway. I haven't got a chance."

"Oh, I don't know," said the English Setter. "You might be surprised. Have a go. It's only a bit of fun."

He lowered his voice. "Take a tip though, old chap. Don't lift your leg. It's not done."

Suddenly Ernest felt much happier.
He gave himself a good shake, and then
when they all began to parade around
the ring, he stepped out smartly at
Sally's side, his long (clean) honey-
coloured coat shining in the summer
sunshine.

Chapter Five

The judge examined each entry in turn,
looking in their mouths, feeling their
legs and their backs, studying them
from all angles, and making them walk
up and down, just as though it was a
class in a Championship Show.

When her turn came, he said to Sally,
"What's your dog called?"

"Ernest."

From under bushy eyebrows Ernest
looked out upon the judge.

"Hallo, Ernest," the judge said, and
then hesitated, because there was one
thing that bothered him. He did not
know what kind of dog was Ernest.

"You don't see many of these," he said to Sally.

"Oh, yes you do. There are lots about."

"Lots of . . .?"

"Gloucestershire Cow-dogs."

"Of course, of course," said the judge.

When he had carefully examined all the entries, he made them all walk round once more, and then he called out the lady of the Manor with her German Short-haired Pointer; but when they came eagerly forward, trying not to look too smug, he only said.

"I've finished with you, thank you."

And he called out, one after another, the Chinese Crested Dog and the Tibetan Terrier and the American Cocker Spaniel and the French Bulldog and the Irish Wolfhound and, to finish with, the Finnish Spitz, and said to each in turn "I've finished with you, thank you."

Until the only dogs left on the croquet lawn were the English Setter and Ernest.

And the judge looked thoughtfully at both of them for quite a time before he straightened up and spoke to the owner of the English Setter.

"A very close thing," he said, "but I'm giving the first prize to the Gloucestershire Cow-dog," and he walked across to the Vicar whose job it was to make all the announcements on the public address system.

"Well done, old boy," said the English Setter. "It couldn't have happened to a nicer chap."

"But I don't understand," said Ernest. "How could I have won? Against all you aristocratic fellows that are registered with the Kennel Club, and have lots of champions in your pedigrees?"

"Listen," said the English Setter as the Tannoy began to crackle and the voice of the Vicar boomed across the gardens of the Manor House.

"Ladies and gentlemen! We have the result of our Grand Dog Show! It's not quite like Crufts, ha, ha – we do things a bit differently down here – and in our Show there has only been one class, for The Most Lovable Dog. And the winner is . . . Ernest, the Gloucestershire Cow-dog!"

And Sally gave Ernest a big hug, and the judge gave Sally a little cup, and the English Setter wagged his plumy tail like mad, and everybody clapped like billy-o, and Ernest barked and barked so loudly that he must have been heard by nearly every cow in Gloucestershire.

Oh, the excitement of being Ernest!

Look out for more titles in the Yellow Storybooks series:

Emily's Legs by Dick King-Smith

It wasn't until the Spider Sports, when Emily won all of the eight-legged races, that everyone began to ask questions. Then they discovered what was so special about Emily's legs...

Sir Garibald and Hot Nose by Marjorie Newman

Sir Garibald wants to play video games. But he lives in a dark, creepy castle with no electricity. What he and his dragon Hot Nose need is a large sum of money. A reward. So they devise a cunning scheme that doesn't go quite to plan...

Anna's Birthday Adventure by Allan Frewin Jones

It's Anna's birthday and she has received presents from everyone, except Uncle Oscar. Surely he can't have forgotten! He promised her a very special present this year. So Anna sets off in search of Uncle Oscar's tower on a deserted island. It's a journey full of surprises and a birthday she'll never forget.

Princess Sophie's Quest by Jacqui Farley

Rescue a prince! All the princesses at Princess School groan when the teacher announces the quest for that week's homework. All except Princess Sophie, who thinks it will be easy peasy. But all the silly princes she meets refuse to be rescued. Surely there's a prince in danger *somewhere.*

Storybooks are available from your local bookshop or can be ordered direct from the publishers. For more information about storybooks write to: *The Sales Department, Macdonald Young Books, 61 Western Road, Hove, East Sussex BN3 1JD.*